## What is Honor Flight?

**The mission of the Honor Flight Network** is to fly America's veterans to Washington, D.C., to visit the memorials dedicated to honor their sacrifices. Top priority is given to America's most senior veterans — survivors of WWII and any veterans with a terminal illness who wish to visit their memorial.

# Saluting Grandpa

## Celebrating Veterans and Honor Flight

Written by **Gary Metivier**

Illustrated by **Robert Rath**

Foreword by **Tom Brokaw**

**PELICAN PUBLISHING COMPANY**
GRETNA 2012

## Dedication

**T**his book is dedicated to the family of Staff Sergeant **Andy Tolliver** and all families who have sacrificed and are sacrificing to preserve our freedoms.

## Author's Note

**O**n Andy Tolliver's final day with us, I got the chance to talk to him about how he inspired the idea for this book. I told him that through this story — he lives on. He smiled as I offered him my best salute — a final salute to a true American hero.

HONOR FLIGHT
of the Quad Cities

First edition, 2011
First Pelican edition, 2012

*The word "Pelican" and the depiction of a pelican are trademarks of Pelican Publishing Company, Inc., and are registered in the U.S. Patent and Trademark Office.*

ISBN: 9781455617487
E-book ISBN: 9781455617494

*Book design by Robert Rath*

Printed in Singapore
Published by Pelican Publishing Company, Inc.
1000 Burmaster Street, Gretna, Louisiana 70053

# Foreword

**O**ne of the most gratifying rewards of having written *The Greatest Generation* is the unexpected dividend of witnessing veterans from that difficult time sharing their experiences and wisdom with their grandchildren.

Certainly it happened in my family, and from what I am told by so many others, it continues to happen now with great-grandchildren as well.

These are the sinews of American life that make us stronger in every way, and we must relish them. Especially during times of trial and challenge.

In this wonderful book about those relationships, you'll be rewarded with the understanding and emotion that comes with generation to generation conversation and common experience.

Moreover, if you buy it and send to many friends, you'll be helping one of the most rewarding experiences a member of the Greatest Generation can have — an Honor Flight to the nation's capital to witness the memorial to all they did to save the world.

**Tom Brokaw**

"**B**ack straight! Suck that belly in! Lift that elbow!" Grandpa playfully ordered as his great-grandson tried to keep up.

"Grandpa, this is hard," Andrew reached for his old worn baseball glove. "Can't we just play catch?"

"Andrew, you wanted me to show you how to salute," Grandpa said. "If you're going to do it, you need to know how to do it right."

"But I'm only in the first grade," he complained.

"You asked me to show you. Come on, put your back into it."

Just as Andrew got one body part going in the right direction some other body part would go somewhere else.

"Take a break, Andrew," Grandpa said. "We'll try again tomorrow."

**T**hey sat down on the porch. Grandpa did what he always does lately when they sat down — he fell asleep.

Grandpa had been kind of sad lately and didn't have much energy to play. He had been like this since he got the letter from the people with the Honor Flight. Andrew had heard about the Honor Flight in school and really wanted Grandpa to go on the trip. He was proud that his grandpa helped saved the world from the bad guys in World War II. But Grandpa didn't feel like talking about it.

Andrew was sure he would share his stories with him. They were best buddies, after all. But so far, Grandpa kept saying, "Maybe when you are older."

Andrew had hoped the 'salute thing' would get him talking. But it hadn't worked. It just meant more work for *him*.

While Grandpa napped, Andrew jumped up to check the mailbox. There IT was. Another letter with the words "Honor Flight".

"Grandpa, you have a letter," he said just loud enough to wake him.

His lips smacked around like a flopping fish as his eyes fluttered open. He looked at the envelope, and he furrowed his brow.

"Aren't you going to open it?" Andrew begged.

"Maybe later," he mumbled as he stood up, patted him on the head, put the letter in his pocket and walked into the house. Andrew thought he looked even *sadder* than before.

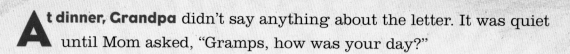

At dinner, **Grandpa** didn't say anything about the letter. It was quiet until Mom asked, "Gramps, how was your day?"

"Fine," was all he said.

Andrew felt frustrated. He couldn't hold it in one second longer.

"Grandpa got another letter today from the Honor Flight people," he blurted out as fast as he could. Grandpa crinkled his forehead.

"That's great!" Mom said. "You are going right?"

"I don't think so," he answered as he pushed his broccoli around on his plate, He slowly stood up and walked out of the dining room.

"He has to go," Andrew complained.

"It has to be his decision, Andrew," Dad said quietly as he cleared the table.

"I know, but all the other grand-dads get to go. They come home to all those people waving and cheering like we saw on the news. My Grandpa deserves that, too."

"He sure does," Mom said. "But, like your teacher told you, some veterans don't want to remember their time at war."

"But, I'm his buddy," Andrew said putting his plate in the sink. "He should at least talk to *me*."

The next day, right after school, Andrew rushed upstairs. He wanted to know if Grandpa decided to go on the Honor Flight. Grandpa was sitting on his bed looking into a big suitcase. It was filled with old black and white pictures, letters and a cool uniform with a bunch of medals and ribbons on it. But when he saw his great-grandson — he closed it with a *snnnaaaappp!*

"So, Grandpa, are you going?"

"Your Mom thinks I should. I've been thinking about it all night. What do you think, little buddy?"

"Sure! You get an airplane ride. Maybe some of your friends will go too?"

Grandpa looked at one old picture that he was still holding. Andrew figured the people in the picture were his friends from the war.

"You know what?" He scrunched his eyebrows. "I think I'll take your advice. I'm going on that trip!" He reached out and gave the boy a big bear hug. "You can help me pack."

B zzzz...bzzz...bzzzzz...
the alarm clock yelled.

"Hey, big guy," Mom poked her head in the doorway. "Time to take Grandpa to the airport."

Andrew jumped out of bed and slipped into the pile of clothes Mom set out for him the night before.

At breakfast, he thought Grandpa looked different. His eyes were looking down and his hands were shaking as he spooned in his boring-looking cereal.

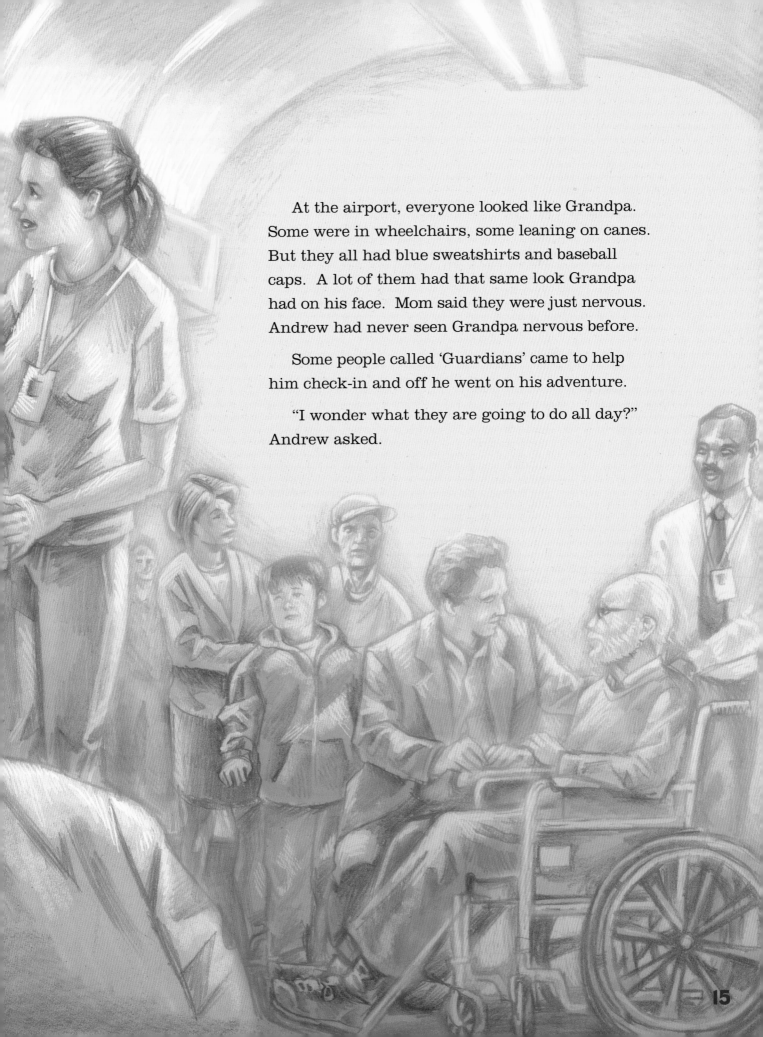

At the airport, everyone looked like Grandpa. Some were in wheelchairs, some leaning on canes. But they all had blue sweatshirts and baseball caps. A lot of them had that same look Grandpa had on his face. Mom said they were just nervous. Andrew had never seen Grandpa nervous before.

Some people called 'Guardians' came to help him check-in and off he went on his adventure.

"I wonder what they are going to do all day?" Andrew asked.

"**Remember the story** we saw on the news?" Dad asked.

"Oh, yeah," Andrew answered excitedly. "People meet them when they land there and show them all the cool stuff."

"That's right," Mom added. "And they will spend the day seeing all of the monuments built to honor all of our veterans. Grandpa will be very tired when he gets home tonight."

At home, Andrew had work to do. He wanted to practice his salute. He wanted it to be just right when his Grandpa and his friends came home that night.

**10** o'clock at night, way past his bedtime,
Andrew was back at the airport.
It was packed with people. Most of them were
holding flags. There were big flags, small
flags — some people were even *wearing* flags.
Little kids slept on the floor or in chairs.
Andrew was wide awake.  He missed his
Grandpa too much to sleep.

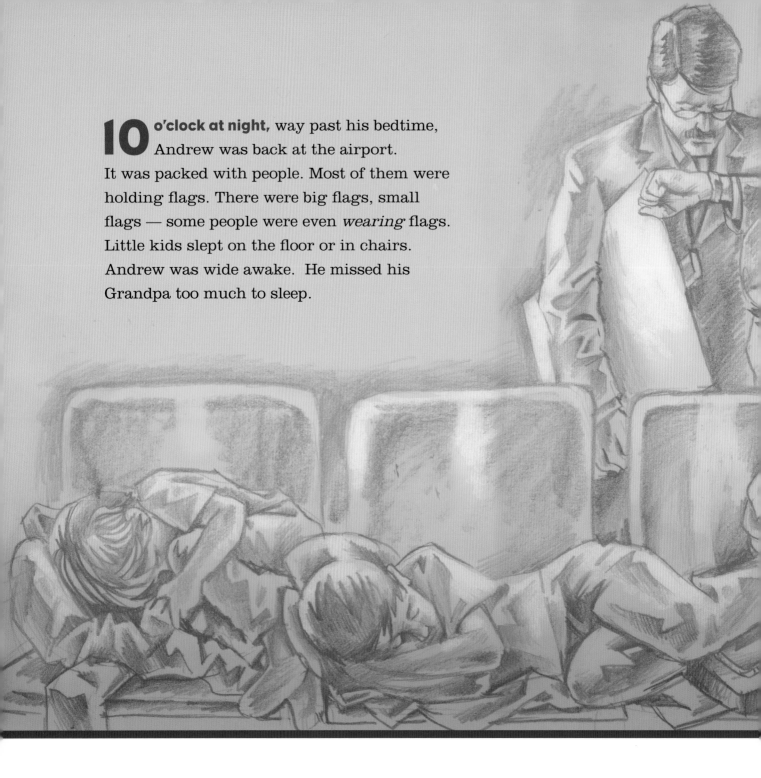

A funny sound got
everyone's attention.
"That's the sound of
bagpipes," Mom
whispered.

**A** booming voice followed.
"Ladies and gentlemen,
please welcome home
the greatest generation!"

Everyone started cheering, clapping,
and saluting.  The men and their helpers
walked right down the middle of all these
people. Some of them wiped tears from
their eyes.

**A**ndrew looked for Grandpa. He could barely see through all the waving arms and flags. He climbed up on a chair and stood on his tippy toes.

"There he is!" Mom pointed. She was crying too.

Grandpa looked through the crowd and spotted the boy on his chair.

**A**ndrew stood up as straight as he could and put his arm up for the best salute he could give. Grandpa stopped in his tracks and stood at attention, too — saluting him right back.

"**N**ice salute, Soldier!" Grandpa said as he reached over and gave him a big hug, lifting him up off the chair.

Andrew noticed a teardrop on his face. "Grandpa, are you sad?"

"No, I'm not sad," he answered. "I'm very happy. I am happy I went on the trip and even happier to be back home to all of this," he looked at the crowd of people.

"**B**ut most of all," he poked a finger gently against Andrew's forehead. "I am glad to be home to you."

"How about we head for home and grab some ice cream along the way? I have some stories of the old days I would like to share with you and your mom and dad. Tomorrow I need to get back to work on my fastball. Whatdaya think?"

"That would be great, Grandpa!"

The next day, the family gathered in the living room. Grandpa had a surprise he wanted them to see. He came downstairs with that old suitcase. He opened it up on the table and started taking things out.

"This was my favorite hat," he said, putting it on Andrew's head.

"And these guys were my best friends during the war," he said as he showed his photos.

Full of energy, Grandpa started telling them about his service.

Andrew was excited. He was so glad to finally hear the stories. But there was one question he just had to ask.

"Grandpa, was my salute good enough? Is that one of the reasons you are smiling?"

"It was just perfect," he said in a booming voice. "It was the best salute I have ever had!"

# Reactions from veterans, volunteers, and family about Honor Flight

"I could hardly believe the crowd that met us at the airport, thanking us, shaking our hands and hugging us. THANK YOU and your staff for an emotional and never-to-be-forgotten day."

**Earl Kerke**

"Anyone who went through that line as a veteran, guardian, or volunteer who did not at the very least have a lump in their throat and a huge smile on their face is an emotionless person."

**F.M. Meersman**

"Thank you and your team for one of the best days of my life. The homecoming was wonderful, never felt so important in my whole 85 years!"

**Don Christopher**

"Even more emotional than V.J. Day was some 60 years ago. Many, many thanks."

**Frank Roberts**

"My terminally ill dad, Clarence Hinke, marveled at perfect strangers thanking him for his service. The greeting at the airport was so emotional; it brought tears to both our eyes. That couldn't have happened without your wonderful group of people and the generous support from the community."

**Diane Derganz**

"The greeting of all greetings was on the return to the Quad City International Airport in Moline and the crowd that was waiting for us there. I guess I waited 64 years for that."

**Charles Robert Delahun**

"I am proud to be a free English speaking American all because of you! I cannot thank you enough for your bravery, dedication, courage, and valor to saving our country. Your efforts stand unmeasured. I hope these memories today will last a lifetime."

**Volunteer Jodi Slingsby**

# A Note from the Honor Flight Chairman

**O**ne of the very first things we discovered when Honor Flight first began is just how important and life-changing an event it would be for our Senior Heroes. Never could we have imagined that a simple trip to Washington, D.C. to see the World War II memorial would influence not only the veterans and the guardians, but their entire families as well. This book clearly illustrates what a significant event this trip really is.

What began as a flight for twelve World War II veterans in six tiny aircraft has now grown into dozens of flights for thousands of the most humble and patriotic people God ever created, now traveling by tour bus, 747 jets, commercial jets, recreational vehicle caravans, and trains. Those thousands of Heroes now understand just how respected, revered, and loved they are by the entire nation. And because of this experience, these veterans now feel comfortable, for the first time in their lives, to share the stories they have held locked in their hearts since 1945. As a result, their families now have the opportunity to learn firsthand what life was like when their Grandpa was a young, strong, bullet-proof (so they thought) soldier on the adventure of a lifetime.

Every Veteran having this special trip returns from it convinced that it is one of the greatest days of his or her life. Comparable to the day they returned from Japan or Europe, comparable even to the day they were married or had their first child. It is truly a remarkable transformation from just a simple offer of kindness and gratitude from the American public.

Every child reading this book or listening to it being read by their Mother or Father will be changed forever. They will never again look upon an aging parent or grandparent as OLD. The sense of respect so long absent from our culture will be reborn as it was in past generations. These amazing senior heroes are truly the 'Greatest Generation'.

And nowhere will it be more obvious than when young children are given the opportunity to 'Salute Grandpa'.

**James A. McLaughlin,**
**Chairman**
**Honor Flight Network ™**

*If you can read this... Thank a Teacher.*
*If you can read this in English... Thank a World War II Veteran!!*
*Before it is too late.*

# How to Contribute

For more information about Honor Flight or to contribute, please visit:

www.honorflight.org

www.honorflightqc.com

# THE BIG BOOK OF
# B MOVIES

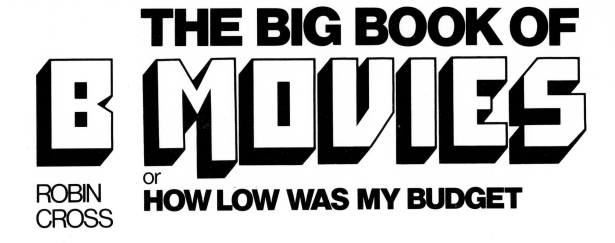

# THE BIG BOOK OF
# B MOVIES
ROBIN CROSS

or
## HOW LOW WAS MY BUDGET

a Charles Herridge book
published by

**St Martin's Press**
**New York**

## Picture Credits and Acknowledgments

All illustrations are from the Kobal Collection, with the
exception of a few from the National Film Archive and the
Cinema Bookshop. Acknowledgments are due to the
following film companies: Allied Artists. Allied Pictures
Corporation, American International, ABP, Anglo
Amalgamated, Astor Pictures Corporation, British Lion
Films, Cinemation Industries, Columbia, Criterion Film,
Continental Pictures, Eagle Lion, Embassy Pictures, Eros
Films, Excelsior Pictures, Fanfare Films, Film Classics
Incorporated, First National, Gloria Film, Grand National,
Metro Goldwyn Mayer, Monogram, New Line Cinema,
New World Pictures Inc., Paramount, Panda Films, Pathe,
Producers' Releasing Corporation, Rank Film Distributors,
RKO Radio Corporation, Republic Pictures Corporation,
Screen Gems Inc., Screen Guild Productions, Tigon
Pictures, Twentieth Century Fox, United Artists, Universal-
International, US Films Inc., Vitaphone, Warner Brothers,
Warner Pathe.

## Author's Acknowledgments

The author would like to acknowledge the help of the
following in preparing this book: Sheila Scott, Suzanne
Greene, Jo Stoner, Jenny de Gex, Ed Gray, Reginald
LeBorg and the staff of the Scala Cinema, London.